Inhale My Thoughts

Author's Remarks

Creativity is the offspring of the mind; therefore we are all products of our thoughts. This book is giving you the opportunity to interact with a place people don't normally go to, my mind. We are all involved in a similar battle just with different people, at different times, and a different place. As you read each word and verse, allow it to paint a picture in your mind. With that being said take a deep breath and **Inhale My Thoughts**.

Ideal Results Books

1st Edition
Daquan Henry

Thank you to all my supporters:

God, Tiesha Henry (Mother), Jason Stafford, Stephen
Stafford, Hector Rojas (Cover Illustrator), Dijay
Chung, Shemuel Pagan, Marcus Jean,
and everyone else who had an impact on
my life along the way

CONTENTS

Wonder Woman

Mommy

Mom

Ma

There's so much to say

I know where to start from

Him not being man enough to handle the wheel

You taking over!

Moving to the driver seat from shotgun

Putting in long hours for us to survive

Drunk off ambition

Determined to keep your future alive

Your faith is still strong

Up until this day

All you had to do was hold on

Allow God to lead the way

Not an ounce of void active in my heart

You kept me fulfilled

Had everything under control

Common job

Daquan Henry

Apply for one position
End up playing more than one role

My apologies
For providing you with headaches
It frustrates you
When I sell myself short
I have the ability to conquer life
But I continue to fail in this sport

I know what I have to do
Changes have to be made
So we can leave this chapter alone
Move on to the next page

I wish I could make you a man from scratch
Good luck!
Finding a good one out of the batch
I will never let a man hurt you
You know guys stop loving early
Hopefully you get someone
Who's love doesn't have a curfew

Things are going to get better

It can't always be a beautiful day
Life has it's sunshine
But there are several storms in the way
Since June 23, 1991 530 p.m.
All you have done was work no play
Today's June 23, 2013
Now it's my turn to carry you
The rest of the way

Our relationship is something
People will never understand
The impossible is possible
Remember
A "woman" taught me how to be a "man"

Changing Roles

Girl I'm the jealous type
Do you know why?
We started as friends too
Randomly got close
A door that we didn't think could open
Three words that wouldn't be spoken

We were friends
Nothing more
Nothing less
Who knew we would be writing
Each other's name on our chest
I used to give you advice about men
Tell you to love yourself
You're not the problem, it's him

I was always there for you
Every graduation
Celebrating
Anytime you were elevating

I can't forget about

The nights you were depressed
Crying on my shoulder
While I held you against my chest
As you vented
I positioned
Myself to listen
A moment of silence
Your present condition
Tempted me to get violent

Now things have changed up
We're together
I'm excited every time
Someone brings your name up
I've been giving you all of me
Promising you a bright future
So you could forget about your past
Doing my best
To be better than your last

So our good times can outweigh the bad
Appreciating what I have
Before it changes to what I had
Most guys will use friendship to cover up

Daquan Henry

Their real intentions
Play the role as a friend now
Later on start doing things to you
They didn't mention

Girl I'm the jealous type
It's nowhere near overbearing
It's just at times I'm over caring
We've been through some tough chapters
I would never want
Our story to be over
Babe I'm just skeptical
If I'm your man
Who's your shoulder?

Born A Leader

God
I think it's time that we sit down and have a talk
Standing tall holding a lot on my mind
With limited time
These massive problems can't be solved
By clearing my head while I walk

I know this isn't the first time you've heard this
With countless blessings
You planted me on this surface
Can you please tell me what's my purpose?

I'm searching for some clarification
Am I here to motivate minds
Who can't encounter ambition?
Provide guidance to the ones who are lost
About to result to submission

It would bother me to stand here
Quietly watching
I feel the need to be heard

Daquan Henry

Far from average
Most people live off nouns not verbs

New to leadership
I'm no vet
Will die spreading the truth
I'm a high risk threat

Surprisingly, I'm far from nervous
I don't mind leading the crowd
At times it's difficult to handle my thoughts
I'm forced to think out loud

I'm only human
I know you won't give me more than I can handle
That type of mindset will leave me ruined
Before I put an end to their scandal

Building my army
With individuals who are willing to learn
Anyone can be a leader
They just can't hesitate to take their turn

God help me!

Inhale My Thoughts

Produce a plan

While I look at the big picture in every angle

Even the Devil had an Angel

Daquan Henry

4 years later

The image of you still dwells on my mind
Claimed I was over you
It says otherwise on the walls
Where you left my heart confined

Don't know who I'm angrier with
You for leaving my life too soon
Me for not pushing
My pride aside to make room

Too comfortable living in your sunlight
At night I forgot to be your moon
In the past I had to remind you about your worth
You haven't received that love from anyone
I know it really hurts

So amazing what an individual's ego can do
Blind me for too long
Ignoring the fact that I really love you

I just want my ex back

We've never crossed paths
But if we did
I would give my next back
Sent you old emotion
Didn't receive a text back
We've been over for years girl
I expect that

Quite some time before you departed
The foundation of my boxing career started
Had a few fights which I won
Fought for respect
Confidence too
My most valuable fight has never existed
I've never fought for you
Until now

Food For Thought

If we all just focus
We can save the souls of the soulless

Give homes to the homeless
If you notice the closest are the coldest

Their goal is to leave us goal less
The ones that are oblivious don't know this

God's Angel

I must say
I'm far beyond impressed
Lost for words
I've interacted with many women
I believe I've encountered the best

She blew my mind
Definitely shocked me!
How could a grown woman exist?
In a young woman's body

She's considerate
About things most females wouldn't be
Sees the solution for the problem
Most females couldn't see

During our first conversation
I could feel her purity
Talk about spiritual
It's like God was raising her
Her parents just had authority

Daquan Henry

I wasn't running from love
Somehow her mind caught me
I've always been priceless
Somehow her aurora bought me

It was a pleasure crossing paths
Hopefully
A good girl won't get broken
We all know the aftermath

Conspiracy

We remain civilized
While our eyes
Lost focus on the political street gang at large
Majority of humanity are oblivious
To the war we are in with the ones in charge

Less violence more silence
It's far from a physical fight
To become victorious in this battle
We have to get our mental right

We are unaware of their actions
Are we foolish?
Are they beyond slick?
It's a new era
For centuries getting away with murder
Using the same old tricks

Being ignorant
Delusional
Is a terrible mixture
Put the pieces of the puzzle together

Daquan Henry

Acknowledge the big picture
Do you comprehend what I'm saying?
Or am I talking to myself?
Will you join me for this march for freedom?
Or am I walking by myself?

A Poem For My First Love

I used to be mad at the world
Doing my best wasn't enough
If I still ended up losing this girl

I'm accustomed to the outcome
It was always the same
I had enough love for you to love yourself
It didn't make a difference
You didn't love yourself!

The low self esteem
Started from your Mother and Father
No affection was provided in the household
If your creators didn't believe in giving heat
Who else can you run to when you're cold?

Only you or your parents can change that
You ran from me to your ex
Allowed insecurities to bring the pain back

Daquan Henry

I'm not angry at you for leaving me
It's the individual who you left me for
You have the key to happiness
But continues to use the right key
For the wrong door

It's sad to say for you to open up your eyes
Something drastic has to happen
Then you'll get tired of getting treated like a Soldier
Move up to a Captain
He did things to you unheard of
There's nothing wrong with forgiving someone
The problem is produced once you forget

My love for you is real
There was no scheme behind the scenes
At night I cuddle with insomnia
To prevent you from showing up in my dreams

This is coming from a man
Who wants nothing but the best for you
Run from his abuse
Before he destroys what's left of you

Black is Beautiful

Ladies
Black is **Beautiful**
I was told to remind you
For a while now
You have allowed the media to define you

My **Caramel**
Brown Sugar
Chocolate Nubian Queens
Did you forget where you came from?
Placed brains on the back burner
Made beauty the main one

Why are you degrading yourselves?
Once they started advertising the chains
You started enslaving yourselves

Forget about the title
That's a dead end
A closed door
Why would you settle?
If you can get more

Daquan Henry

Than you have been bargaining for

When I look at you
I see a masterpiece
Something much greater
I need you to realize it now
Not tomorrow
Not years later

I'm searching for
Self confidence
Self value
Self respect
You will go far in life with just that
Stop saying you're a mixed race
In all reality you are only black

This was a topic that needed to be discussed
Rosa Parks put her life on the line for a reason
Not for you to place yourselves in back of the bus
Eliminate the media's opinion
Put yourself first
Right now you're placing who you are
In a hearse

Value yourself

By any means necessary

Inherit your worth

It's hereditary

Daquan Henry

The Chosen One

My boxing Brother
People wonder
Where did you get your name from
First off
Life has hit you
With some strong left hooks
Immediately after you came back
With a counter right
It takes will power
To be the counter type

You're built for survival
Using the ring as your chess game
Using the proper technique
As your shield
You're someone's idol

Amazing Speed
Penetrating Power
Agility
Everyone isn't granted those abilities

Not once did you allow
Your ego to speak for you
People talk about you
More than you talk about yourself

You don't care about the fame
You don't care about the wealth
You were chosen for a reason
Your talent wasn't meant for anyone else

There are so many distractions
Maintaining discipline
Is a challenge in our world
From the
Streets
Drugs
To the
Girls

Everyone is not a fighter
Anyone can wear the boxing attire
To make it to the top
You have to carry
Discipline, Dedication and Desire

Daquan Henry

You have been
Investing time with our youth
Directing them in the right path
Helping them find confidence
Locating their other half

Immaculate defense
Still can take a hit
Definitely a born Champion
It's taking our society time to realize it

Insecurity At It's Finest

Her mind lives in her own insecurities
Her confidence is an unborn baby
Undeveloped
Inactive
Alive for a short period of time
Never got to experience the fresh air

The appearance she carries is ART
In it's purest form
As she presents her presence
Living her everyday life
Men dress her up with compliments
Without hesitation
Their kind words are stripped down
She sees them as non winning lotto tickets
They have no value

When I look at her
I witness the scars
Dug so deep
It is unseen to the human eye

Daquan Henry

Her cries are so silent
Yet so loud
I can't do much in this situation
This consistent battle is hers to fight
Only one problem
She is fighting herself

She thinks that I hate her
I don't
I hate her thoughts
Her self esteem
Her negative comments
The source of her insecurities

I don't want her time
Her money
Her emotion
Her Body
I just want her
To love herself
So hopefully in the future
I can do the same

What Makes Me Different?

What makes me different?
I might read more
Ran away from everything that's artificial
I choose to be pure
Assemble my words wisely
Before I allow them to be released
Avoid the violence
Focus on peace

What makes me different ?
I believe in integrity
I won't compromise my virtues and values
For money
Or to become a celebrity
I don't think twice
The second thought just confuses you
I know the value of everything
I pay no mind to the price

What makes me different ?
I only try to impress
The people who matter the most

Daquan Henry

Not the ones that appear
When you're successful
Trying to make a toast
I'm grateful for my life
I don't forget where I've been
I pray for my enemies not only my friends

What makes me different?
I love helping people
Without looking for a reward
Or any recognition
From the goodness of my heart
Not under any conditions
I will rebuild the bridge
Before I let it burn
I will stop jealousy in his tracks
Patiently wait my turn

What makes me different?
I don't always agree with Webster
I have a different meaning of royalty
I remain humble
I value loyalty
Bragging doesn't excite me

What makes us the same?

We all have

1 heart

1 brain

206 Bones

Red blood

Emotion to care

This is why our world is chaotic now

All we do is compare

Mind Blowing

It all started with a kiss
A touch on the table
Lips touching her navel
She wasn't able
To stay stable

There was no stopping
From her throbbing
Her legs in the air
It went from muscle spasms
To organic orgasms
Without using no magnums

Only the power of the lips
She started to feel more excited
Couldn't help to fight it

To beg for another climax
I didn't need any feedback
To see that
Mind Blowing Sex
Was something she needs back

I just wanted this to be her best
With her chest against my chest
Legs wrapped around me
Dripping in sweat
While I'm kissing her neck
While she screams "oh yes"

Daquan Henry

Overprotective Girlfriend

Girl
Why are you protecting him?
Without even protecting yourself
You know that you deserve better

Stop allowing love to drown you
One day the Paramedics
Won't be able to bring you back
You will be gone forever

I see that you're stuck on the past
When he treated you as a Queen
An illusion
Definitely a trap
First few months were beautiful
Overtime happiness and you
Started forming a gap

I admired the old you
Your laughs
Smiles
Positivity

When it's all said and done
I'm not here to say "I told you"

You seem to have
Too many long nights
Too many tears
You can't hide
Those stains on your pillow
Even though it's sunny outside
I always find rain on your window

Keep telling yourself
Things will get better
Without an actual date
He's never brought anything to the table
Not even the plates

What's between his legs
Doesn't make him a man
You are still dealing with a boy
Years after puberty
He still wants to play with toys

Makes you feel low

Daquan Henry

To feel high
Drains your energy
So he can survive
You have to dead him
So you can become alive
Can't force him to walk straight
When he has a thing for curves

Chemical Reaction

I've never knew this
You can fall for someone
Off of one kiss
Two lips

Maybe that's the reason why
It's hard for me to digest
So I digress
To take away my stress

For you not being here
Reasons why I'm not seeing clear
All I wanted was
To begin where you begin
End where you end

When I see you with him
It's hard for me to pretend
To not feel a certain way about it
So I go a certain way about it

The moment

Daquan Henry

When you started sinking back
I started thinking back
How long have you decided?
Our love would have collided

I guess I was misguided
To believe
You would never leave

Told you what I wanted
Didn't you tell me to be specific?
Now my tears are analogous
To the Pacific
Wow I've never knew
Love is so scientific

In My Own Element

As my body soaks
My thoughts float
In this beautiful liquid

Messages
Get delivered to me
Crevices
In my mind
Get filled up

It soothes
Removes
The stress I let build up
Feeling so high
Problems can't bug me
Gravity can't hug me

My surroundings
Heighten
I feel enlightened
My quest for answers is over

Daquan Henry

Finally found the portal
Less than three seconds
Went from a human
To being immortal

Ear drums stop beating
I develop tunnel vision
Such a deep insight
Never knew that this was possible
Who knew?
The key to life is all physiological

Dear, Good Men

Forgive us for taking advantage

Wasting your time

See when God blessed us with your presence

We weren't in our right minds

Effected by a series of bad relationships

Too much heart break

Caused us to be emotionally drained

We've never got to see the beauty of love

Only the ugly side attached with pain

Our emotions didn't get caressed with sunshine

Only smacked with rain

Which motivated us to constantly say

Love's name in vain

Deep down through all of the anger

We are beautiful people inside out

Our hatred for love is so strong

Even Cupid is on the hide out

Do you know what it's like

Crying all night?

Cheated on more than once

Ignoring anything he has to say

Swearing you won't take him back

Daquan Henry

But you do anyway!
Valuing someone else's happiness more than yours
Searching for the entrance to a man's heart
Constantly trying different doors
Allowing him to be a man by taking the lead
Demolishing our social lives to meet his needs
Battling all types of abuse
Breaking down our self esteem
Blinded by love
Confusing this tragedy with reality and a dream
Every male we encountered
Was searching for a handout
We admit that we've made some bad choices
For some reason
The heart breakers never stand out
GOOD women gone BAD
Our patience ran out
Love is no football game
The goal is
For it to go the distance
Without an end zone
Us women have a bad habit

Placing the good men in the friend zone

Our deepest apologies

We are really sorry

Sincerely,

The Women that deserve true love

The women that deserve true love

P. S. have patience with us, it takes time to heal

It's difficult to trust anyone

When you're used to getting the short end of the

deal

Living the lives of women who are scarred

Running from love is our way of taking it hard

Daquan Henry

Seduced by Suicide

She was a Goddess
With a pain
Full of darkness
So harmless

A person who was
Once vulnerable
But now heartless

The hardness
Made her realize
The less she talks to her conscience
The less she'll start to feel self-conscious

Consistently blaming herself
Men taking advantage
Is her form of relieving herself
All because she forgot the feeling
Of believing in herself

This miss has been misguided
Misleading herself

Now instead of the men
She's the one!
Who's mistreating herself

The truth is
Where the proof is
She thinks the pain will go away
If she acts more ruthless
Damn
How foolish

Daquan Henry

Self Development

For this crime I have committed
No court room is needed
There's no way I could win this case
Outnumbered by evidence that can't be deleted

So I plead guilty
Guilty for not acknowledging my blessings
Only constantly counting my problems
Sitting against the wall depressed
Instead of brainstorming ways to solve them

Life is a challenging math equation
I already have X
Now I have to find Y
To get out of this situation

People view me as the motivator
The guy with positivity
At times I get tired of chasing her
So I end up replacing her

Inhale My Thoughts

I spend time with negativity
For the fact that
Her attention is easy to acquire
She holds me
For as long as I want to be held
Her love for me doesn't change
Even after I have failed

I end up breaking away from her
She's no good for me
That devilish charm
Her depressing vocal
Prevents me from expanding my horizons
Keeps me local

I can't stay away from positivity
She's the blood that my heart pumps
The thoughts that my mind is married to
I definitely admire her
The foundation of my success
Why would I fire her?
We all need a break from our spouse
I won't allow
The distance to be persistent

Daquan Henry

In the long run it will only hurt
She will help me stand up
When my legs don't work

Quality over Quantity

Call me weird
But I get turned on more
By a woman's intelligence than her appearance

It's breathtaking when
She can teach me something
I don't already know
Or hold a intellectual conversation
Longer than it takes the sun to go down

I want her to drown me
With her ambition
So in the afterlife
I'm inspired to generate opportunities for myself

I want her
To reveal only a small part of her body
Leave it to my mind to undress the rest

I want her
To make me earn everything
Her Mind

Daquan Henry

Her Body
Her Soul

Dead-end

Have you ever been faithful
But single?
When the person
You adore
Ignores

You get that feeling
Of fighting a war
That isn't yours

But of course
You feel it more
When they
Treat you like floors

Then your scars
Start to determine
Who you really are

Daquan Henry

To My Future Son

Son
Listen up
Everything that I am about to tell you
I need you to tune in
Don't allow arrogance
To move in

My goal is
To raise you to be a man
Keep
Integrity
Leadership
Intelligence
As your number one fans

I will teach you
Not to collect condoms
Like action figures
And actually use them
Show you that crying and weakness
Aren't identical twins
People tend to confuse them

Enlighten you on being
A provider
Mentally
Emotionally
Physically
Financially
Women need all of the above
Most guys believe
Sex and money is enough
That's not love!

Install in your body
To not put abuse to use
I will invest in your education
At the end of the day
All you have is your mind
If your eyes aren't synchronized
With your brain
It will cause you to be blind

I will encourage you
To build opportunities
Not problems
When you do encounter some

Daquan Henry

You will have knowledge
On how to solve them

Push you to use
Someone else's successful situation
As your own inspiration
I will be there for you
Every step of the way

I will show you how to be a man
Not how to pretend
Being a "man" is something
A "boy" can't comprehend

A Love & Hate Relationship

Love
I love you
But I hate you

You're too dominant
Too controlling
Can't have a dinner date with my mind
Without you getting jealous
I'm aggravated by your bipolar ways

One minute
I'm your man on the moon
My feelings for you
Are beyond this planet

Next minute
I'm drowning
In my own emotion
You leave me breathless
Dehydrated
From all the tears that abandoned my eyes
There are days you let me bond with tranquility

Daquan Henry

With you
I don't feel like a man!
You don't fight fair
Last night I got ambushed by estrogen
Looking for some testosterone

Why are you so beautiful?
Giving my skin
My eyes
That sunset glow

Why are you so draining?
Sleepless nights
Constantly manipulating my vision
Had me following
A path that I couldn't even see

Too many occasions
I have put out a restraining order against you
Then I stopped it

I've realized
I'm the one!
That can't stay away from you

Can't stop stalking you

Can't stop craving your presence

I just want to taste the air that you breathe

Caress the ground that you walk on

Love

I love you

But I hate you

Ego Effect

What have I lost besides you?
Definitely the tender loving care
From deep inside you
Swam away from your heart's current
Also the tides too!

I'm debating
Still waiting
For a better day
Should've divorced my ego
Then asked my heart for a better way

You know how guys are
We don't ask "how to" questions
Inquire about directions
We get lost
Continue to drive far

I'm ready!
Ready to push my ego aside
Encourage my feelings to roam free
Many have tried to get close to me

Those other women had to be copies
If you're the original key

It may be too late
Better late than never
It's time to put down my guards
Allow our situation to get better

Higher Learning

Standing in front of intuition's door
Look at where my mind has brought me
Who can I trust?
Me, myself, and I
Time has taught me

If I'm searching for the truth
The news is the last place where I would find it
Knowledge is retained
While only the lies remain
They only release what they want you to know
Been guiding you since the zygote stage
Heading in the direction
Where they want you to go

Dig deeper than deep for the evidence
The modified school curriculum is irrelevant
I used to be delirious barely getting by
Constantly being curious opened my third eye

Started reading more

Stopped flicking through the channels
Started seeing more
Understanding the scandal
Being stuck in a warp of distraction
Made life hard to handle

12 years of schooling
Never once did they mention who's ruling
What am I learning?
College Degree
Working 40 hours weekly for 40 years
Retiring with less than 40% of my benefits
What am I earning?

Marketing is all psychological
Credit card companies sending every card possible
Encourage me with alluring words
So I can feel inspired immediately max out
Then the interest rates
Will have me in a submission hold until I tap out

Strayed away from the contaminated food
I understood it was detrimental to my health

Daquan Henry

Planning an escape from modern day slavery
Realized a job is detrimental to my wealth

Time is being wasted every time that I blink
Catching up to my destiny
All I had to do was **Free My Mind And Think**

Spiritual Alarm Clock

Every morning I am awakened by you
I rise out of bed so easily since you tempt me
Your essence gives off vibes that you're present
While you wake me up gently

I appreciate everyday that I am awaken
This gives me a chance for new opportunities in life
Postponing the date my life will be taken

Looking forward to this special day
I'm following the path to see you
While your spirit leads the way

As I stand in front of you
My hand caresses
From your tombstone to your grave
Shed more than a few tears for you
Allow my emotions to become your slave

Vulnerable right now
The memories are causing my mind not to behave
It's wandering off to places

Daquan Henry

I don't want it to go
Forcing me to inhale pain
My sensitivity to grow

Damn out of all the individuals on earth
Why did I have to pay?
They say perfection doesn't exist
I guess God made that opinion a fact
By taking you away
I've heard time heals
Hopefully things get better
Before I leave you
My mind drops two flowers on your grave
Those are the only roses that live forever

Wishing I could have seen it coming
Maybe some type of notice or sign
I assume both of us was waiting to meet death
You were just on the front
I was on the back of the line

What To Expect From Me

I release a love
Beyond skin deep
Focused on accessing
Where her blood is pumped
Where her thoughts sleep

I'm here to play my role
If it's needed
I will guide you
Anyone can have
A beautiful exterior
I want what's inside you

I'm your best friend
Your enemy's enemy
Living in your mind all day
Your memory's memory

Daquan Henry

My Escape

Today
At this very moment
I will give everything up
Just to escape

Can't depend on anyone
I have to be my own hero
Wear my own cape
Found a place much greater
Where materials are meaningless
Baby Blue skies
A paradise in disguise

Joyful people
The ground is gold
The offspring
Of the earth is enjoyed
Happiness never gets old

They have no assistance
No money
That's a bad mixture

Some how through the negatives
They find a positive in the picture

I crave to be there
Every second
Every hour
Every day
For now I have to patently wait
Hopefully
The good doesn't come too late

I'm far from selfish
Anyone who's searching for paradise
I will lead them
Money can buy anything
But it can't buy freedom

Daquan Henry

The Definition Of Love

What is **Love**?
In one Word
Support

Make me feel unstoppable
Prevent me from being close minded
Refuel me with motivation
Before my tank gets empty

Be my umbrella when it rains
Be my body armor
Blocking out the pain
Show me
That our relationship is unconditional
Be my other leg when I lose balance

Be my backbone
When the rest of my body malfunctions
If we are losing signal
Help us establish a connection
Keep my eyes on the windshield
Not the rearview mirror

Inhale My Thoughts

Motivate me to be all I can be

Help me eliminate my fears

Be the evaporation that absorbs my tears

Help me channel

My anger

My pain

My sorrow

On to paper

Instead of allowing it to surface the universe

Be complete

Be a whole

So we can be two wholes

Two difficult to separate

If I need blood

If I need an organ

If I need positive thoughts

Give me yours

I have no problem

Giving you mine

If I need a heart

Then you haven't been taking care

Daquan Henry

Of mine since I gave it to you

When I ask you
What is **Love**?
Don't tell me
Show me

My New Type

My new type
Is my type
Meaning if I'm your type
You're my type

So if she's "A" type
I can't be "B" type
We share the same heart type
If we share the same heart type
We share the same blood type

Like AB type
So my new type
Is my type
Meaning if I'm your type
You're my type

Daquan Henry

Envy's Empire

Loyalty
The word is still alive
The meaning is extinct
I've never had a large circle
Three friends at the most

First One
Was wounded by my success
Third degree burns
Telling me how he's proud of me
How I'm blessed

I got him his first job
My intentions were helping him succeed
Instead of being grateful
He wanted to make sure
I wasn't in the lead

He had a problem
With every girl I talked to
He would make smart remarks

It was subliminal hate for me at heart

Would eat everything I had offered him
But watch me starve
Six years of friendship
It took me time to notice
I was in denial
He cut me off quick
Right when I was putting him on trial

Second one
Eight years I've known him
The same amount of time
Envy has owned him
He hid his jealousy well in disguise
Never attempted to support me
First one looking for me to share my prize

He's the type to abandon his friends
When a woman is present
When their relationship is over
He will crawl back as if nothing has happened
If you see any pictures with him

Daquan Henry

Remove loyalty from the caption

Every girl I talked to
He would tell his friends to pursue them
He didn't care
Tell me how she's not a good investment
Everyone owns a share

He's the type
Who would sleep with my Girlfriend
My Wife
Breaking all the rules
Tell me that he pushed her away
She made the first move

Pathological liar
Devilish actions
If I'm dying
Why would someone that's trying to compete with
me?
Have some compassion

I'm far from angry
I'm aware karma is going to get him

Inhale My Thoughts

I cut him off quick
He didn't even know what hit him

Third one
Seventeen years going strong
We work together against life
When things tend to go wrong
He stands for loyalty like no other
Thank God that my Mother
Didn't have to go through nine months of pain
To give me a Brother

We've been through some tough situations
Street fights
Getting jumped
Not once did he run on me
Since day one remaining calm
While battling storms
Up until now where I have the sun on me

One thing I know
Being disloyal won't take you far
I don't have to state any names
You know your traits

Daquan Henry

You know who you are

Disappearing Acts

You'll show me love now
Then later
Make me feel like you hate me

I'm confused
Being with you
Did I win?
Or
Did I lose?

I've given you everything
But my soul
If you could
You would take that too
Even though it's impossible
You would break that too

Of course I get tired
Tired of the crying
Tired of the lying
There are times
You make me feel

Daquan Henry

On top of the world
No worries
No stress
No competition
Other days
You put me down
Your love comes up missing

I'm curious to know
Out of all people
Why you?
I'm your body guard
All I've done was stand by you

I'm definitely your plan "A"
The plan that you gave up on
The relationship that lost it's beauty
You didn't bother putting makeup on

I can't take it anymore
Once I turn that corner
There is no turning back
I've never been in to magic tricks
Your love keeps playing Disappearing Acts

Love & War

Girl we're fighting a war
We both can't even win
Attacked by my own thoughts
Thoughts of you leaving
Sending each other mixed emotion
Without valid reasons

If we walk away
We're both going to lose
Separation
Or
Elevation
We shouldn't have to choose

I've never had any doubts
It was always to death do us part
I'm only human
You can't expect me to live without my heart

We can't end it now
There is definitely a chance
Of things getting better

Besides

We are nowhere near forever

Note To Dad Part 2

What has been going on?
Have you been drinking?
Drunken mind
Sober thoughts
Does it have you thinking?

Out of nowhere you want to reconcile with me
You auctioned off your manhood for sell
Can't sleep at night
Reality is eating away your brain cells

Now you're searching for a peace of mind
I believe you just want a piece of mine
For you to come around
There has to be a reason
After someone else's work is done
You're the type to reap the benefits
Tax Season

Stop wasting your breath
Enough of your excuses
Enough of your lies

Daquan Henry

Déjà vu all over again
I've already heard it
Here you are acting innocent
When the jury had already read their verdict

If you place my Mother in harm's way
I will kill you myself
Develop last minute amnesia
I'll forget how to dial 911
You're better off calling hell for help

Forcing a man to be a man
That's one tough situation
Father's Day has been expired
I don't accept late applications

Do us a favor
Keep your distance
Forget about being persistent
This is my last response
It doesn't matter what you do

I'm done
There's no point of my Mother and I

Fighting a battle that we've already won
You're only making your life harder
Any **Man** can be a **Dad**
Any **Boy** can be a **Father**

Daquan Henry

I Want You

You're so beautiful
You will never understand
What your eyes did
I just want to count
Every eyelash on your eyelids

Feel your heart beat
Your inner rhythms
Swim deep within
So you can envision
My inner vision

Beauty from the neck up
Not necessarily
Facial features
But your mind
A much greater feature

I just want you to
Follow your heart
A much greater leader

Lost Love

It went from texting all the time
To getting no replies
Looking in to each other's eyes
Now looking at each other cry

Not enough answers
Too many excuses
Not enough love
To the point it became obtrusive

How can a relationship go from being
Priceless to Lifeless?
Peaceful to a Crisis?
Silence to Violence?

Love
The word you were trying to show me
It's crazy how you used to hold me
Now you act like you don't know me
Should've just told me
At least that's what you owe me

Daquan Henry

Military Madness

Damn
I've really messed up this time
Gave them permission
To strip me of my freedom
Wearing a uniform
That suffocates the breath
Of everything freedom stands for

A bully on steroids
We have
The money
The power
The land
But we demand more

This camouflage uniform
Is conflicting with my positive spirit
It holds
The screaming souls of the lost soldiers
If you stop being oblivious
You can hear it

Listen closely
As their constant cries mold me
Paying me with warning signs
They feel that they owe me
In each patch holds their faces
Which are locked in
I signed the dotted line
Now I'm boxed in

Watching
My future just pass me by
They told me
You're not here to think
Just do what your told
There is no asking why

My first mission is
To eliminate my brain
Deal with the pain
Risk my life
For your financial gain

I have
1 heart

Daquan Henry

5 senses

Emotion

But you want me to be inhumane

I'm too intelligent

Don't forget physically fit

They went from

Persuading me

To

Degrading me

Slaving me

Once I physically quit

Those colors

That we painted our surroundings with

Comes with the wrong definition

Greed has always been the CEO

Freedom, honor, respect

Weren't even granted a entry level position

I woke up just in time

Selling my soul

To reach my goals

Damn I wasn't in my right mind

Inhale My Thoughts

I apologize to my Mother
My absence made pain present
Made you suffer
It's a fact
I was obligated to take a tour on war
The 400,000 life insurance wouldn't bring me back

It took me to wear that camouflage attire
To obtain a deeper insight
Realizing I wasn't ready for heaven
I was about to send myself an earlier invite

Civil War

Too many times
My mind and heart
Battle each other
Back and forth
Constant Civil War going on
South and North

My mind
Births logical thoughts
My heart
Can't stay calm
Runs with open arms
Recklessly

Chasing love with no plan
That's neglecting me
You have to realize
There's no "I" in team
If your main focus is protecting me

You just want to be loved
That's so cliché

I want tomorrow
To be a mystery
Not my history on replay

Daquan Henry

Unpredictable

The Question is
Do I know what tomorrow holds?
My life can be in order
Moments later randomly unfold

Gun could go off
Stabbed to death
I'm diagnosis with a disease
Now my life flashes before me
As I drop to my knees

Deep breaths
Motivating blood to circulate through my veins
As my heart is ceased
Blood leaves
Pushes my body's temperature
To drop down in degrees

While time runs out
Several questions run through my mind
Did I deserve this?

Inhale My Thoughts

Did I fulfill my purpose?
With me gone
Will my family be fine?
Did I leave enough money behind?

My funeral arrangements are irrelevant
I could care less about my remains
They attempted to control my mind and body
It's my Spirit that can never be tamed

I'm far from perfect
I don't try to be
People get fed up
When I discharge positive energy
After they've tried to pry the negative out of me

Having a good heart can become an issue
Aggravated Assault
It bothers them when every time someone sneezes
I'm willing to provide a tissue

I'm too happy
Too intuitive
Too generous

Daquan Henry

Someone didn't like the way I was moving
I wasn't in search of a W
Must mean that my lifestyle
Placed them in the position of losing

I'm not afraid of my surroundings
I'm afraid of the people that surround me
The ones that show me love on the daily basis
If they plan something
No who, what, when, where, why or how?
They won't leave any traces

Everyday I question
If life and I are on the same speed
I could see Heaven tomorrow
If Hell gets tired of my good deeds

Living Thoughts

If we started to spend time together
And
I began to fall in love with you
I wouldn't make an attempt
To catch myself
The temporary pain
The bruises
The scars
Would all be worth it

I'm angry at you for being you
You're so high up
I'm too short to reach you
So I will keep trying
Until you start dropping obstacles
In my direction
That only means
It was never intended
For us to establish a connection

As I stand here
Watching your beauty develop

Daquan Henry

Hopefully some of your traits
Will fall on some of these women
Down here within my reach

You have me
Wanting to stay asleep
Avoid waking up
The truth is
The dreams I have of you
Stomps on my reality

Genocide

I wake up every morning angry
Frustrating to see where we're heading
200 miles per hour to a dead end
God I'm praying for an Armageddon

Racial profiling by the demons in blue
Programmed to attack now
Ask questions later
We are guilty of those actions too

It's sad
How you want to keep my life and body distant
Black on **Black** crime is consistent
We allow white on black crime
To sit in front of the bus
But it's no different

Killing our people as if there is no tomorrow
Producing too many funerals
Not enough graduations
Having one night stands with the truth
Marrying fabrications

Daquan Henry

The system was created for us to fail
Considered a felon
Without stepping foot in jail
Stop knocking on the door of extinction
Within time someone will answer

My Brothers and Sisters admit that you're lost
Let me help you
My support is being offered at no cost
My mission is to move at your speed
I have no intentions on stopping your progression
Fighting for the lead

Tomorrow is not promised
Any second I could be gone
I'm a homeless man hungry for change
**I am Martin Luther King, I am Malcolm X, I
am Sean Bell, I am Trayvon**

No Room For Patience

As soon as we locked eyes
I felt a vibe that was new to me
Love at first sight
Damn what did you do to me?
My eyes told you everything
Things my lips weren't ready to express
I'm aware that you have to return to heaven soon
Please hold open the gate for me
I can't have you right now
So do me a favor
Wait for me

When I gaze at you
I see my future
Standing right in my presence
Second hand smoke from your positive energy
Floating on cloud 9 off your essence
You're craving my love
Vice versa
There's one reason why we can't be together
I never get the women that I want
People may think it's a coincidence

Daquan Henry

I feel it's fate for me
I can't have you right now
Do me a favor
Wait for me

I offered to just be your friend
You rather keep the distance
Instead of getting too close
Then putting our bond to a end
I pray for you more
Than I pray for myself
Ambushed by selfish thoughts
Don't want you to end up with someone else!
So close to being with my soul mate
Obstacles had to get jealous
They ended up building hate for me
I can't have you right now
Do me a favor
Wait for me

Years later
You have a Husband
Two children
An unstable marriage

Inhale My Thoughts

A family

Your face lost it's golden glow

He planted his seeds

Forced them to grow

He took for granted

Everything that I desired

My plans for us got murdered

Shots fired!

You got distracted

While holding the gate for me

Damn girl all I needed was one favor

All you had to do was

Wait for me

The Detox

As the sun rises
I face the usual
Morning madness
Smothered by laziness
Morning traffic

Within these last few weeks
My focus has shifted
Started worshiping time
Treating seconds
As if they resemble days
Determined to succeed
Brainstorming different ways

Spending less time
Searching for acceptance
Spending more time investing
Using confidence as a weapon
Fighting against all failure
Still facing obstacles
Life's interceptions

Inhale My Thoughts

I had to remove people from my life
Ones that didn't deserve their position
Bringing me down indirectly
Only by my side under certain conditions
Preventing their darkness
From reaching the light
Darkness may be dark
In certain weather it shines bright

Some people find
Their own happiness in their friends
Misery loves company
I find my own happiness within
Life doesn't come with instructions
At times I don't know where to begin
This is where faith comes in

I've cleansed my circle of toxins
At least the ones that I've noticed
There are plenty more to come
I'm waiting for anyone to give me a reason
There's one mandatory detox each season

Daquan Henry

Our Final Conversation

You lost me with
We both knew
It wouldn't work
We took the risk anyway
Believing it wouldn't hurt

You had the nerve to say
I will find someone else
The same way I found you
The whole situation made me angry
Those words brought me down too

I rather be a complete stranger
Than watch our relationship hit a dead-end
Then I'm the one in the closet
Left on a hanger

It's better to shut it down now
Before it gets too deep
My reality will be aligned
With my nightmares
There's no point of going to sleep

Inhale My Thoughts

Visual is worse than audio
I rather hear about your marriage
Instead of seeing it firsthand
Another guy taking a permanent spot
Of being your man

I can't be your friend
I can't be in the background
Watching someone else
Have what I want
Have what I've worked for
Have what I deserve
Have what I know I would appreciate

From this moment on
I don't want to occupy
Any of your thoughts
Leave them vacant for important things
Things that are connected to your future
We both know
I'm not one of them

Deadly Diamonds

Deadly diamonds
Deadly diamonds

Damn

Dangerous

Diamonds

Dealt

Death

Developing

Dancing

Demons

Declaring

Destruction

Dishing

Dominance

Defeating

Defenseless

Dehydrated

Delicates

Deadly Diamonds
Deadly Diamonds

Darkness

Destroyed

Dawn

Designing

Devils

Discoloring

Dudes

Despite

DNA

Desiring

Diamonds

Melanie

Let me tell you about a girl named Melanie
I could feel her pain
You can hear it through the melody
Melanie
Never really cared for fidelity
Only for the fellows who's influenced by felonies
Especially someone
That will always put her secondly
Her existence will come to a end eventually

It's ironic how an analyzer
Can love a womanizer
I had to ask myself
What is this world coming to?
She told me to stop judging

The things she released to me was unbelievable
My frustration just continued to pile
I couldn't understand
How a man
Raising his right hand
Do this to their child?

Inhale My Thoughts

She started talking about her Father
Who she really hated
How she stood there and waited
Waiting to get violated
While her eyes dilated
Every time she was getting annihilated

There was definitely no excuse
For the heinous sexual abuse
She's never ran in to love
She's only ran in to lust
She was never rescued
Only abandoned by trust

Her life pushed anger to hold me
As she stood here and told me
How she kept her cries inside
Right after darkness and her life collided
I'm sitting here listening to
A beautiful face with an ugly past
I've watched this same movie before
Starring a different cast

I don't know how to help her with this battle

Daquan Henry

This is a tough fight here
I know every second she's hoping she might hear
The blaring sound of her alarm clock
Waking her up from this nightmare

To My Future Daughter

As your Father
I only want the best for you
Since your birth
I was granted the job
Of protecting you

I will educate you on a man's thoughts
The truth won't be sold separately
Usually the lies are only bought

I will love you unconditionally
Teach you everything that I know
Start you on your journey
Shower you with
Love
Affection
Watch you grow

Raise you to be a woman
Install self respect
Promote you to love yourself
Watch you crawl

Daquan Henry

Help you up
Every time that you fall

Allow you to stand up
Walk on your own
But remember
You will never walk alone

I will always be there
Until my life has fraternized with submission
I will still be there
My spirit will take over the position

I won't put you on lockdown
It will only drive you crazy
I won't give you unlimited freedom
It will only make you have a baby

I will give you
Freedom with boundaries
I know balance is key
I will be your eyes
Until you're able to see

Make sure you get the upmost fulfillment
Show you how to be
Mentally
Physically fit
In life you have to be resilient

I will be an example
Of the type of man
You should invest in
I will be more than a Father
I will be your Dad

Daquan Henry

Caught by Cupid

How do you know when you're in love?
When their hugs are the drugs
You can't breathe or sleep without
They are constantly on your mind
Until there's nothing else to think about

You place their happiness before yours
Allowing that person full access
Opening all doors
Making sacrifices to please them

Your trust for them is too strong
Pushed off the cliff by lies
Still having the ability to hold on
Drained from the pain
Having an affair with depression
Using your mind more than words
Second guessing

Your family
Your friends
Telling you that you deserve better

You believe that person is more than enough
Your facing a temporary storm
Assuming it will go away if you remain calm

On the road to heart break
Feeding yourself lies
Removing all of the exits
Leading to your own demise

Daquan Henry

Overlooked Knowledge

Do you want to know?
Why we don't reach our dreams
"Fear" stops you
"I can't" drops you
In to an average lifestyle

Working a nine to five
Constantly complaining
Angry at the world
Then we get a second job
Since we are barely maintaining

As time passes by
Jealousy is born
Instead of asking for help
We will invest
Forty hours in a job
Forty hours watching TV
But not forty hours in ourselves

Attention all
We have been

Brainwashed

Programmed

Fooled

For centuries

Doing the same old routine

Spending our whole check in ten minutes

Living beyond our means

We don't know any better

We've never learned about

Investments

Savings

Stocks

Bonds

We are setup to

Graduate

Work

Get married

Then we're gone

There are two types of income

Linear

Residual

Daquan Henry

One will make your dreams a reality
The other will keep it as a visual

Can't forget about social networks
Our biggest distraction
Leaves you on ready
But you will never get to action

My advice
Set goals for yourselves
Give yourself a dead line
Running around without a plan
Of course you're going to fall behind

Only you
Can make your shackles loose
Your alarm clock
Woke you up to go to work
It hasn't woken you up to the truth

My Perfect Woman

I would love for her to be gorgeous
I rather her mind match her appearance and be
flawless
Loves me hard
Knows when to give me space
Compliments my strengths
Pinpoints my weaknesses
Believes she can't be replaced

Turns her back on gossip and rumors
Knows when to be serious
Also has a sense of humor
Independent, Goal oriented, Supportive, Mature
Values my love
Doesn't go outside our relationship looking for
more

She releases a love that is so pure
Won't stress over her imperfections
I'll appreciate her every flaw
Doesn't allow life to leave her blinded
She listens

Daquan Henry

She trusts
Carries the traits of someone who's open minded

Understands me better than no other woman will
Has no problem expressing how she feels
Doesn't follow the crowd
Builds her own path
Influences me to be a better person
Plays the role of my other half

Even with all the obstacles we encounter
She knows how to control her temper
Locks me in her heart once I enter

A woman that's original
So unique
Can make me nervous at times
Leaves me to the point
Where I can't even speak

Constantly grasps my attention
Introduces me to something new
If I'm not meeting her needs
She shows me how to

Far from possessive

A little aggressive

Can accept a challenge and propose one

When times get rough she won't flee

Realizes no one is perfect

But she is perfect for me

Lost Thoughts:

What happened to value?

I remember when the smallest things were considered valuable. When females made guys earn everything, their time, affection and body. This was the same exact era when holding the hand of the person you were attracted to, meant the world to you. In addition, you were smothered by butterflies in your stomach due to the excitement of the physical bond you have just established. At that moment it was confirmation for you to believe he or she was yours.

I remember when kissing was utilized to express the passion you felt for someone. The "kiss" was a language your heart spoke in which your mind couldn't recognize and convert in to words. As you leaned forward, closed your eyes, and tasted their lips you felt your heart race to the point where you thought it was going to jump out of your chest, but at that moment you didn't care.

I remember when sexual intercourse stemmed from
passion; it was more than just a physical desire.
Long before you took off each other's clothes you
were already naked when you revealed your most
precious thoughts, secrets, fears, and imperfections.
Everything that makes you who you are was shared
with that person and your body was the last piece to
the puzzle. The sexual tension was so powerful that
your mind already had an orgasm but your body was
waiting for it's turn. It was amazing how you could
hear their heart race through the noise; between the
heavy breathing, eye contact, goose bumps, and
moaning. The whole experience was treasured,
priceless and unexplainable.

Love vs. Race & Religion

What is Love? Love is a beautiful disaster; it is a creation that is developed from two people who have mutual respect, affection, appreciation, infatuation and much more. This couple places their significant other's happiness before their own and is willing to make sacrifices for the benefit of the relationship. Sounds amazing right? Well, it isn't always pleasant; it can encourage you to feel like you're on top of the world where everything in your life is going right even when things are going wrong. In addition, it has the ability to emotionally and mentally drain you. There are times love makes you angry, sad, and crazy. Love has two sides Heaven and Hell, the side that you interact with the most all depends on which one your relationship caters to.

Do we have the right to place limits on love? No, we don't! Love is love; you can't disqualify someone from being your soul mate candidate just because they're a different race or practice a different religion. Love is emerged from compatibility which is beyond our control. One of the major reasons why people don't invest in someone outside of their race or religion is due to the fact of their parents, family, and friends being disappointed in them. In some situations I've seen families disown a person for doing what they feel is right. To my knowledge all religions stand for love and unity. If someone judges you for making an attempt to be happy, they are going against their religion. We are all human; we weren't designed to be perfect. Ask yourself this: If your family or friends judge you, is their love for you genuine? Does concealing who you are and who you want to love make you happy?

4/23/2014

A Letter To Women

Dear Ladies:

What I am about to tell you is not meant to mortify you. I want to encourage you to love yourself; to reach your full potential not only as a woman, but as a person. For years now, I've noticed that you constantly degrade yourself. Whether it's exposing your body on social networks, walking outside with little to no clothes on, or simply conducting yourself in a way that people perceive you lack self-respect. Yes, most men fall in love with what they see, but only temporarily until another woman captures their attention. If a man is only interested in you based on your physical features, he will only be with you until he gets bored or is ready for a long term commitment. Honestly, in his mind that's not a category you fit in to. When you expose your body, automatically we assume that's all you have to offer. You and I know that's not true. Here's some advice you may not want to hear but need to; stop dedicating all of your time to display your outer beauty over your inner. The truth is physical attraction will only lead to sex, nothing more. After sex, don't be surprised if he runs out the door faster than he helped you take off your clothes. If you don't know your own worth how can you expect someone else to? With that being said why do you grant men the ability to take advantage of you?

Another thing, you have been investing more time in one night stands, friends with benefits, and having a few boyfriends just to prevent yourself from getting hurt. The mindset that you keep is "all men are the same" and you can't trust them will be your downfall. Ladies all men are not the same, you just have a bad habit of choosing the same type of guys. If this applies to you, my advice is to keep your head high, your standards even higher; stand by them by any means necessary. You have to love yourself more than anyone else! Stop trying to find love within your friends as well as any man who gives you attention. If you don't know this by now, let me be the first to tell you, men are going to chase you down regardless whether you expose yourself physically or not. I want you to stop trying to change a man; think about how difficult it is to change yourself, and then you will realize how difficult changing someone else is. It doesn't matter what I want, you have to want it for yourself. We all know you don't like running from love and would rather be in a relationship. Do yourself a favor, and stop running, exercise better judgment when it comes to the man you choose to invest time in. Time is such a precious gift, one you can never get back so don't waste it. I hope this letter touched you where your thoughts sleep, where most guys don't take time out to acknowledge. There is no perfect manual that reveals "how to keep a man" because every man is different but may have similar characteristics; at least make him respect you along the way

Sincerely,

A Real Man

A Real Man

P. S. Remember BE CONFIDENT and when it comes to your body "the less revealing the more appealing". Allow a man's mind to take a trip and wonder....

www.ingramcontent.com/pod-product-compliance
Lightning Source LLC
Chambersburg PA
CBHW071926220626
47052CB00002B/482